Goodnight, Sweet Pig

To Peyton, Shaela and Brianna Barney, with wishes for sweet dreams — L.B.

To Luc, for all his support — J.M.

Kids Can Press acknowledges the financial support of the
Government of Ontario, through the Ontario Media Development
Corporation's Ontario Book Initiative; the Ontario Arts Council;
the Canada Council for the Arts; and the Government of Canada,
through the BPIDP, for our publishing activity.

Published in Canada by
Kids Can Press Ltd.
29 Birch Avenue
Toronto, ON M4V 1E2

Published in the U.S. by
Kids Can Press Ltd.
2250 Military Road
Tonawanda, NY 14150

www.kidscanpress.com

The artwork in this book was rendered in acrylic.
The text is set in BeLucian Ultra.

Edited by Debbie Rogosin
Designed by Marie Bartholomew
Printed and bound in China

This book is smyth sewn casebound.

CM 07 0 9 8 7 6 5 4 3 2 1

Library and Archives Canada Cataloguing in Publication

Bailey, Linda, 1948–
    Goodnight, sweet pig/written by Linda Bailey; illustrated by
Josée Masse.

ISBN-13: 978-1-55337-844-0 (bound)
ISBN-10: 1-55337-844-X (bound)

I. Masse, Josée II. Title.

PS8553.A3644G65 2007   jC813'.54   C2006-903045-6

Kids Can Press is a l'orus™ Entertainment company

Goodnight, Sweet Pig

Written by Linda Bailey   **Illustrated by Josée Masse**

Kids Can Press

To sleep, or not to sleep? That is the question.

1 Pig number one was trying to sleep, plumping her pillows and counting sheep.

2 But pig number two liked to read with a light and eat buttered toast all through the night.

3 Pig number three liked to watch TV
and paint her trotters and drink iced tea.

4 Four was a boar who juggled with plums.

5 Five came to bed with a full set of drums.

6 Six was a pig who loved to bake —
he brought an enormous birthday cake.

7 Seven showed up in a wedding dress and stepped in the cake. Yeeks, what a mess!

8 Pig number eight was a Spanish dancer.

9 Pig number nine was a Bengal Lancer.

10 Ten was a famous basketball star who brought his whole team in a luxury car!

Pigs on the pillows!
Pigs on the floor!
Pigs in the closet!
Pigs at the door!

The first little pig began to weep,
"How can a poor pig get some sleep?"

She asked them all, in the sweetest way,
if they would kindly . . . go away.

The other pigs were badly shook —
for pigs are nicer than they look.

10 Ten wiped a tear from his famous snout and took his team and tiptoed out.

9 Nine said "Sorry!" and offered a ride

to pig number eight, and they pranced outside. **8**

7 Seven took out a mop and broom and tidied up the messy room.

6 Six brought clean sheets for the bed and pillows for the sleepy head.

5 Five read a gentle bedtime book — short, but that was all it took.

4

Four gave a tender kiss goodnight.

3

Three turned out the bedside light.

2

And number two sang lullabies